ABDO Publishing Company is the exclusive school and library distributor of Rabbit Ears Books.

Library bound edition 2005.

Library of Congress Cataloging-in-Publication Data

Metaxas, Eric.
  The monkey people / written by Eric Metaxas ; illustrated by Diana Bryan.
     p. cm.
  "Rabbit Ears books."
  Summary: The people in a village in the Amazon rain forest grow so lazy that they
eagerly allow a strange man to create monkeys from leaves to do everything for them.
  ISBN 1-59679-226-4
  1. Indians of South America—Colombia—Folklore. 2. Monkeys—Colombia—Folklore. [1.
Indians of South America—Folklore. 2. Folklore—Colombia.] I. Bryan, Diana, ill. II. Title.

F2270.1.F6M47 2005
398.2'089'98—dc22
                                                                    2004059467

All Rabbit Ears books are reinforced library binding
and manufactured in the United States of America.

ABDO
Publishing Company

The MONKEY PEOPLE

WRITTEN BY ERIC METAXAS   ILLUSTRATED BY DIANA BRYAN

RABBIT EARS BOOKS

On the edge of a beautiful, round lake, deep in the endless rain forests of the Amazon, there was once a very prosperous village. As more and more children were born into their midst, the villagers built more huts, and as if by themselves, their humble gardens and herds of goats grew and grew. Nothing could have been better or easier for anyone. Even the many fruit trees that grew wild in that region seemed to flourish, producing larger and sweeter and more colorful fruit than at any previous time in their history.

And because all went so well for such a long time, the people of the village began to neglect certain things that their forefathers had taught them, such as cleaning up after themselves and repairing what was broken. And in time they had quite forgotten what it was like to do anything at all.  And so now, when things got dirty or fell into disrepair, they simply elected to move and leave their difficulties behind them. So they would stay in one spot until the mess grew to great proportions: The rotting fruit grew into great heaps and the huts let in more rain than they kept out. And then they would move to a new spot and build new, even flimsier huts. Over the course of several years their antipathy toward work pushed them counterclockwise around the lake. One day they found that they had traveled all the way around to the very place they had started. And it was then and there that they decided to stop moving altogether, for moving about was quite tiring in its own right.

O ne day, however, late in the after-noon, a strange thing happened. As the villagers were lying in their hammocks complaining about how sore they were from lying in their hammocks, a mysterious series of smoke puffs appeared across the lake.  It was difficult to make out their source, and everyone had grown so exquisitely lazy that even squinting was to them a laborious chore that irked them considerably and made them roll their eyes with impatience. Naturally no one considered the possibility of walking around the lake to investigate, for that would have required a walk of nearly a quarter of an hour. Instead, they sat in their hammocks and tossed about various lofty possibilities, until after many hours they arrived at an exceedingly clever alternative. You see, they hit upon the idea of selecting a small child among them, one whose eyes were very sharp. They would carry this eagle-eyed cherub to the very top of the tallest tree in the village so as to give him the very best vantage point possible, and he would tell them what he saw. That way no one would have to trudge around the lake, and they would still be able to determine the source of the mysterious smoke. It was settled.

Ah, but immediately there were various complications. To begin with, one of the villagers had made some calculations, and he informed them that since they must carry the child to the top of the tallest tree in the village, they must also be sure to select the very lightest child possible, else it would be far too much work carrying him. Another of them determined that they should carry a newborn child into the tree. They could then bring him down and wait until he was old enough to tell them what he saw. After all, what was the great hurry? Huge debates raged as various pros and cons arose—and then pros and cons for each of the pros and cons—and so on and so forth, until great schools of thought had grown up around the issue and everyone involved was quite sure that everyone else was quite wrong.

And if the truth must be told, and in the end it must, let it be known that the particular child they selected was less a product of their long philosophical debates than of the relatively simple fact that little Tepe was not afraid of heights. When the child had been carefully carried into the highest branches of the great tree, everyone in the entire village waited at the bottom and all throughout the lower branches to discover the slightest nuance of what he saw.

Finally, the child was brought down, but he was quite young and for whatever reason he did not speak for some time. Everyone had their eyes focused on his mouth so intently that at one point when he hiccuped, an old woman clutched at her heart as though the heavens themselves had opened.  When at last he spoke, everyone learned that the puffs of smoke they had seen came from the pipe of an old man who was sitting on the other side of the lake, and that with a knife he was cutting large leaves into the shape of monkeys.

But this only piqued their curiosity more than ever about who the man was and why he was doing what he was doing. And the debate that now followed was a grand, overweening structure of many stories that went up and up and nowhere, high into the sky. 🐒 As they were carrying on amongst themselves, little Tepe wandered away from them and around the edge of the lake to where the man was seated smoking his pipe. Before anyone noticed that the small child had gone, he reappeared in their midst, holding the old man's hand. 🐒 Now the people of the village were quite amazed at the old man's presence, but the old man hardly seemed to be aware of theirs. He only continued to puff his pipe and look around at the considerable mess and disrepair with sadness. 🐒 Soon one of the elders of the village, a very fat man, came forward. "Well now!" he said. "We have come to understand that you cut leaves into odd shapes, eh?" 🐒 "Yes," the old man replied. 🐒 "Well? What do you want from us then?" the elder said impatiently. "I hope you do not expect us to finance your hobby by buying them from you. We are very busy here, you realize. We have precious little patience with peddlers." 🐒 The old man only scratched his head and smiled. "No," he said, "I do not wish to sell them. In fact, you can have as many of them as you want."

With that he put his fingers in his mouth and whistled a loud, low whistle that carried to the other side of the lake, and in no time four odd-looking monkeys—that seemed very much like little men with long tails—came scampering all the way around the lake, arriving in the midst of the people. 🐒 "Ah, yes," the old man said. "As you see, they come to life after I release them from the various leaves which they inhabit." He smiled. "And they are quite capable of every and any task imaginable. How many would you be requiring?" 🐒 Now the villagers just stood there trying to take this all in. They were not a little astounded that the man was able to cut figures that sprang to life, but their amazement was quickly eclipsed by an overwhelming desire to somehow use this old fool's naive generosity as a way to avoid work. 🐒 "Well, there isn't much around here we can't do ourselves," replied the elder craftily. "You see, we're quite happy and self-sufficient—but just to please you we will take as many of the hideous creatures as you need to get rid of." 🐒 "As you please," said the old man. "Take them all. Perhaps they could be best occupied cleaning up these piles of rotting fruit." And no sooner had he spoken this than the strange creatures commenced doing that very thing.

N ow this pleased the people immensely, for the village had never been in worse condition, and they certainly had not planned on doing anything about it themselves. And when they saw that the monkeys were moving along smoothly, they immediately went to lie down in their hammocks, for the commotion of the day had been for them, on the whole, rather tiring.  As they did this, the old man just sat down and continued cutting large leaves into the shape of monkeys. Those of the villagers with enough energy to peek beyond the tranquil horizon of their hammocks observed that as soon as the figures left his knife, they indeed came to life and stood at attention, awaiting his orders.

After a time, a thought stirred in the mind of the obese elder, and he returned to the old man who now had several new monkeys in front of him. "Seeing as how you have these creatures standing about idly," the elder said, "perhaps we might borrow them to fetch water for us, or firewood perhaps?"   "As you please," the old man said, and in no time several of the monkeys were occupied carrying water from the lake and fetching firewood from the forest, and everything proceeded smoothly.   But it wasn't long before the villagers were rubbing their hands with anxiety again and complaining about other chores that they had to do. "It would certainly be nice if we weren't constantly occupied hunting game and digging roots, and if our women weren't occupied cooking meals and feeding the children all the time. What a chore those things are! And how tedious!"  "Yes, indeed!" chimed another. "It would be so wonderful if we were free to pursue our thoughts. That's a far purer occupation, don't you think, than digging roots and wiping children's chins? If that ancient leaf-cutter is so keen on helping us, why can't he provide those services as well?"

And so they went to the old man, who had another row of newly minted monkeys standing in front of him. "See here, Grandpa," they said to him, with more energy than they had displayed in months. "We're perfectly willing to work—that's not the issue! But we believe that man cannot be happy doing the things that are best fit for lower beasts. We are not cut out for menial chores. You see, we're thinkers and philosophizers by nature. That is, after all, what separates us from the monkeys, is it not?" "As you please," the old man said, and in no time he had fashioned huge phalanxes of monkeys who sprang about and dug roots and picked fruits and hunted rabbits and cooked food and fed the children and did everything that needed doing in the village.

And now, because everything in the village that needed doing was being done, life there changed quite considerably. The people had never had more time on their hands before and so they lay in their hammocks for many weeks on end, sleeping and thinking until days and nights ran together into an uninterrupted gray soup. 🐒 But it wasn't very long before little things began to bother them. They soon wondered why they couldn't have monkeys to bring them their food and monkeys to keep away the flies and monkeys to rock their hammocks ever so delicately! And one of them was elected to communicate this to the old man. 🐒 But on hearing their complaints, he was quite agreeable. "As you please," he replied. And almost immediately there were monkeys rocking the hammocks and leaping up and plucking flies out of the air and other monkeys who carried food from the monkeys who were cooking it to the people in the hammocks. But even now the villagers were not satisfied, and from that point on, they seemed to spend all their time trying to find something to complain about.

Then one day as they were lying there, exhausted from trying to think of something to complain about, a tiny pinprick of sunlight, half the diameter of the finest spider's web, navigated its way through the maze of branches above them, and reached the hammock of one of the villagers. And he reacted just as though someone had poured water on him. "That does it!" he shouted. "That does it! Exactly how does that lazy leaf-cutter expect us to be able to think clearly with this meddlesome old sun poking his nose into our affairs? It's an outrage, that's what it is—an absolute outrage!" Well, this struck quite a resonant chord among those others in the hammocks who were awake, and they quickly nodded their assent to the diagnosis, for they were elated that someone had finally put his finger on the source of their misery. "Yes," one of them said. "It's a wonder we can do any thinking at all! It's a miracle, that's what it is! Couldn't that good-for-nothing old-timer create some monkeys to solve the problem?" And so again they went to the old man and presented the problem. And, as you might expect, in no time at all there were vast squadrons of monkeys poised everywhere in the rich canopy of trees above the villagers' heads. And each one of the hundreds of monkeys held in his paws a large palm frond.

From that point on, whenever a pinprick of sunlight found its way to the hammock of one of the sleeping people in the hammocks below, twelve or fifteen monkeys who were sitting idly in the branches would instantaneously scramble to the spot to blot out the offending beam of light. Now, there are some older versions of this story in which the people demand that the old man make enough monkeys to stand on each other's shoulders and build a tower of monkeys tall enough to reach the sun. Then they could push it back to the other side of the horizon and hold it there—and that way the villagers would be undisturbed forevermore. In those versions, which we know to be perfectly untrue, the old man cut out a monkey whose job it was to cut out monkeys who cut out more monkeys. And no sooner had the old man put the final touches on this first monkey than it came to life and began creating another version of itself. And no sooner had this next monkey come to life than it too began creating a monkey creating a monkey, and so on and so forth.

In no time the place was a frightening mud of monkeys. One couldn't walk two steps without stepping on a tail and getting bitten, and so the planned tower of sunward monkeys simply never got off the ground. 🐒 But of course, that is not how it happened at all. What really took place was that even with all the monkeys in the trees keeping the sunlight out, the villagers continued to be dissatisfied. 🐒 One of them, clutching his stomach, claimed he couldn't think great thoughts because

his digestion bothered him. So the old man carved a monkey who would do his digesting for him. Another complained that he couldn't think great thoughts because he grew sore lying in the hammock, and so the old man carved a monkey to lie in the hammock for him. Yet another man claimed that he would just get a noble and brilliant thought and then he would become conscious of his own breathing and forget what he was thinking about. So the old man carved a monkey to breathe for him. It all became quite ridiculous

Then there came a day, at last, when one of the villagers complained about how sick he was of complaining, saying that the complaining was the thing that kept him from thinking great thoughts. And so he did the only thing he could do—he asked the old man if he could make monkeys who would do the complaining for him. Many others had the same request, and together they brought their requests to the old man. Of course he smiled at this and then, as usual, he nodded, granted. And now, because the monkeys were able to do absolutely everything the people did, including lying in the hammocks and complaining incessantly, things in the village became extraordinarily confusing. For you see, try and try as one might, it eventually became quite impossible to determine just who were the monkeys and who were the people. And it seems that the true answer as to which was which, or who was who, or if indeed it mattered at all at that point, will always be open to

As for little Tepe, in time he escaped to another village where everyone was so industrious and so content that it made one's head swim. And there, riding great swells and tidal waves of productivity, he lived the remainder of his life. He became rather a prolific leaf artist in his own right, and during the course of his life he created entire rectangular universes with his meandering knife.  And when he grew older, he could be seen sitting at the base of a large tree with a tender smile on his face, smoking a pipe and creating this very story in all of its odd shapes and particulars, for anyone who was interested.

THE END